英文小說解讀攻略

冒險篇

戴逸群 —— 主編

Guy Herring —— 編著

三民書局

國家圖書館出版品預行編目資料

英文小說解讀攻略：冒險篇／戴逸群主編;Guy
Herring編著.－－初版一刷.－－臺北市：三民，2021
　　面；　　公分.－－（閱讀成癮）

　ISBN 978-957-14-7167-9　（平裝）
　1. 英語 2. 讀本 3. 中等教育

524.38   110003852

閱讀成癮

英文小說解讀攻略：冒險篇

主　　　編	戴逸群
編 著 者	Guy Herring
責任編輯	范榮約
美術編輯	黃霖珍
封面繪圖	Steph Pai

發 行 人	劉振強
出 版 者	三民書局股份有限公司
地　　　址	臺北市復興北路 386 號 (復北門市)
	臺北市重慶南路一段 61 號 (重南門市)
電　　　話	(02)25006600
網　　　址	三民網路書店 https://www.sanmin.com.tw

出版日期	初版一刷 2021 年 4 月
書籍編號	S870830
I S B N	978-957-14-7167-9

三民書局

—————— 序 ——————

新課綱強調以「學生」為中心的教與學，注重學生的學習動機與熱情。而英文科首重語言溝通、互動的功能性，培養學生「自主學習」與「終身學習」的能力與習慣。小說「解讀攻略」就是因應新課綱的精神，在「英文小說中毒團隊」的努力下孕育而生。

一系列的「解讀攻略」旨在引導學生能透過原文小說的閱讀學習獨立思考，運用所學的知識與技能解決問題；此外也藉由廣泛閱讀進行跨文化反思，提升社會參與並培養國際觀。

「英文小說中毒團隊」由普高技高英文老師與大學教授組成，嚴選出主題多樣豐富、適合英文學習的原文小說。我們從文本延伸，設計多元有趣的閱讀素養活動，培養學生從讀懂文本到表達所思的英文能力。團隊秉持著改變臺灣英文教育的使命感，期許我們的努力能為臺灣的英文教育注入一股活水，翻轉大家對英文學習的想像！

戴逸群

—————— 作者的話 ——————

When I came to Taiwan I taught at Bei Da High School. I met Ian, who has also published a book in this series—*Interactive Reading Guide: Wonder*. At that time he started to have an interest in teaching English through the use of picture books. The school was a testing ground for new ways of teaching, in preparation for the new curriculum. As a primary school teacher in the UK I had experience teaching in a cross-curricular way and I felt I could add my expertise to these new courses. The class I taught there was the testing ground for this book. I have tried to combine the methods I learnt in the UK—teaching many different subjects such as history and geography through the medium of English, while always having a focus on what would work best for Taiwanese students.

Charlie and the Chocolate Factory is a popular book in the UK both for adults and children. Its themes of the underdog and the relationships between adults and children are universal. The students who took my course loved to learn English in an authentic way, not simply from a textbook. I hope you gain the same benefits from this book!

Guy Herring

Contents

	Lesson (pages in the novel)	Activities	Page
1	Meeting the Bucket Family pp. 1–7	Post for Charlie	1
2	Wonka's Factory pp. 8–12	Newspaper Report	4
3	The Indian Prince, Secret Workers and Golden Tickets pp. 12–21	Golden Ticket Diary	8
4	Finding the Golden Ticket pp. 21–26	Different Types of Parenting Styles	11
5	The Chance Is Getting Smaller pp. 26–34	Character Log	14
6	After the Final Try pp. 34–46	Happiness Line Chart	18
7	Getting Ready to Go to the Factory pp. 46–57	Letter Writing	22
8	Inside the Factory pp. 57–68	From Words to Images	25
9	Augustus Disappears and Oompa-Loompas Arrive pp. 68–80	Sing and Sympathize	28
10	The Chocolate River Journey pp. 80–91	Cacao Bean Journey	31
11	Violet Turns Violet pp. 91–102	The History of Candy	34
12	Lifting Drinks and Square Candies pp. 102–109	More Than One Truth	38
13	Veruca Salt Disappears pp. 109–118	Parents' Imperfections	41
14	The Glass Elevator and the TV Room pp. 118–129	PEEL Writing	44
15	Mike Teavee Is Shrunk pp. 129–141	You Are the Director!	47
16	The Only One Left pp. 142–147	Charlie's Profile Page	50
17	The End pp. 147–155	Character Word Cloud	53
18	Overall Review	Book Review and Book Blurb	56
	Answer Key		59

Picture Credits

All pictures in this publication are authorized for use by Steph Pai and Shutterstock.

Meeting the Bucket Family
Pages 1–7

Word Power

1. draft *n.* 冷空氣
2. screw *v.* 旋緊
3. starve *v.* 餓死
4. munch *v.* 大聲咀嚼

5. torture *n.* 折磨
6. take a nibble 咬一小口
7. enormous *adj.* 巨大的
8. belch *v.* 噴出

Reading Comprehension

(　) 1. Where does Mr. Bucket work?
　　　(A) In a candy shop.
　　　(B) In a toothpaste factory.
　　　(C) In a chocolate factory.
　　　(D) He doesn't have a job.

(　) 2. Charlie always gets a chocolate bar for his birthday. How long does he make it last?
　　　(A) One week.
　　　(B) Up to two weeks.
　　　(C) More than a month.
　　　(D) He finishes it on his birthday.

(　) 3. What is the thing that upsets Charlie the most?
　　　(A) His family are poor.
　　　(B) He always feels hungry.
　　　(C) He lives next door to the biggest chocolate factory in the world.
　　　(D) He doesn't get to eat chocolate as much as he likes.

Further Discussion

1. Life is uncomfortable for the Bucket family. How do we know? Give textual evidence.

_____

_____

_____

_____

_____

_____

2. What is Willy Wonka's factory like? Give textual evidence.

_____

_____

_____

_____

_____

_____

3. If you lived next door to Wonka's chocolate factory and could smell it everyday, but couldn't go inside, what would you do?

_____

_____

_____

_____

_____

_____

Post for Charlie

Charlie is posting a photo of Willy Wonka's factory. Write the caption for him.

charliebucket

#willywonka #chocolatefactory
#delicious #hungry #mywish

2

Wonka's Factory
Pages 8–12

Word Power

1. shriveled *adj.* 乾癟的
2. huddled *adj.* 依偎在一起的
3. extraordinary *adj.* 不凡的
4. have sth up one's sleeve 有…絕招

5. absurd *adj.* 荒謬的
6. gobble *v.* 大口吞吃
7. dotty *adj.* 瘋瘋癲癲的
8. eagerly *adv.* 熱切地

Reading Comprehension

( ) 1. What do Charlie's grandpas and grandmas look forward to each day?
    (A) Having time to take a rest.
    (B) Seeing Charlie.
    (C) Eating cabbage soup.
    (D) Going out for a walk.

( ) 2. What did Willy Wonka **NOT** invent?
    (A) Chocolate ice cream.
    (B) Candy balloons.
    (C) Strawberry marshmallows.
    (D) Blue birds' eggs.

( ) 3. Who is Prince Pondicherry?
    (A) An Indian prince.
    (B) A worker in the factory.
    (C) A shopkeeper.
    (D) A friend of the family.

1. If you were one of the grandpas or grandmas, what stories would you tell Charlie to keep him entertained and why?

_____

_____

_____

_____

_____

_____

2. Grandpa Joe describes Willy Wonka as a magician with chocolate. Which celebrity do you think is like a magician at what they do and why?

_____

_____

_____

_____

_____

_____

3. Which of Willy Wonka's inventions do you think is the best? Why?

_____

_____

_____

_____

_____

_____

Newspaper Report

Who is Willy Wonka? What has he done? Imagine you were a reporter interviewing an ex-factory worker from Wonka's factory and finish the newspaper article.

The Great Town Times No. 98765

Revealed: the secrets of Willy Wonka, the chocolate magician

There is a large, amazing chocolate factory found in a small town in the UK. It is the most famous, yet mysterious factory in the whole world. Its owner is a weird, marvelous man. There are a lot of hidden secrets in the factory.

Mr. Willy Wonka is the owner of the largest chocolate factory in the world.

The former factory worker says the cocoa beans they used were of very high quality.

_____
_____
_____
_____
_____
_____

Inside the factory there are many incredible rooms full to the brim with weird machines making the most unusual kinds of chocolate for every type of person. These candies are ones mere mortals could never imagine.

_____
_____
_____
_____
_____
_____
_____

3

The Indian Prince, Secret Workers and Golden Tickets
Pages 12-21

Word Power

1. colossal *adj.* 龐大的
2. pull sb's leg 哄騙
3. stammer *v.* 結結巴巴地說
4. spy *n.* 間諜

5. whir *v.* (機器) 發出嗡嗡聲
6. faint *adj.* 模糊的，隱約的
7. wrapping paper *n.* 包裝紙
8. glisten *v.* 閃耀

Reading Comprehension

( ) 1. What was Prince Pondicherry doing when he found his palace melting?
   (A) Sleeping.
   (B) Swimming.
   (C) Eating.
   (D) Crying.

( ) 2. Why did Wonka close his factory?
   (A) He was deep in debt.
   (B) He was too old to run the factory.
   (C) His competitors sent spies to his factory.
   (D) He decided to pursue his own dream.

( ) 3. What will the finders of the Golden Tickets get?
   (A) A chance to design their own chocolate bar.
   (B) A trip around the world.
   (C) A job for life in the chocolate factory.
   (D) Enough free chocolate to last their whole life.

Further Discussion

1. Why does Grandpa Joe tell Charlie about Prince Pondicherry and his palace? What story have your grandparents ever told you?

_____

_____

_____

_____

_____

_____

2. If you were Willy Wonka, and you knew there were spies in your factory, what would you do? Would you close the factory?

_____

_____

_____

_____

_____

_____

3. If you were Charlie, and you had just read Willy Wonka's notice in the newspaper, how would you feel? What is the first thing you would do?

_____

_____

_____

_____

_____

_____

Golden Ticket Diary

Imagine you found one of the five Golden Tickets released from Wonka's factory. Write a diary about how and where you found it and how you felt about it.

Memo No. _____

Date   /   /

Dear Diary,

_____

_____

_____

_____

_____

_____

_____

_____

_____

_____

_____

_____

_____

_____

_____

_____

_____

_____

_____

4

Finding the Golden Ticket
Pages 21–26

Word Power

1. hooligan *n.* 流氓
2. nourishment *n.* 營養
3. vitamin *n.* 維他命
4. thrill *n.* 興奮

5. revolting *adj.* 令人反感的
6. frantically *adv.* 瘋狂地
7. murmur *v.* 低聲說
8. spoil *v.* 寵壞

Reading Comprehension

(　) 1. What thing do Augustus Gloop's town **NOT** do when he finds the Golden Ticket?
(A) They have a parade.
(B) They give children a day off school.
(C) They hang flags everywhere.
(D) They award Augustus a medal.

(　) 2. What happens to Professor Foulbody's machine?
(A) It is destroyed.
(B) It doesn't work and only finds silver things.
(C) The mechanical arm falls off.
(D) It finds the Golden Ticket and is put in a museum.

(　) 3. How does Veruca Salt find the Golden Ticket?
(A) She buys hundreds of bars and finds it herself.
(B) She finds it in the snow.
(C) The workers in her father's factory unwrap a lot of chocolate bars.
(D) Her father invents a machine that finds the ticket.

Further Discussion

1. Augustus' mother says it is good for him to eat all the chocolate bars because he needs the nourishment and vitamins. How would you explain to her that eating too much chocolate is bad for your health? What foods would you recommend eating that are full of vitamins and nourishment?

_____

_____

_____

_____

_____

_____

2. People put a lot of effort into finding the Golden Tickets. What do they do? Which do you think is the most effective way?

_____

_____

_____

_____

_____

_____

3. If you were Veruca's father and you had a spoilt daughter, what would you do and why?

_____

_____

_____

_____

_____

_____

Different Types of Parenting Styles

Psychologists have found that there are four main types of parenting styles: Authoritative, Authoritarian, Neglectful, and Permissive. To understand their differences, please look at the picture below.

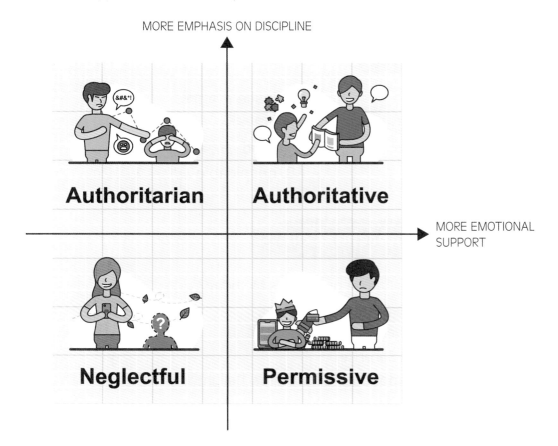

Roughly speaking, Authoritative parents are caring and reasonable. Authoritarian parents are very strict. Neglectful parents pay little attention to their children, and Permissive parents spoil them.

According to the definitions above,
1. what type of parent is Augustus' mother?
    ☐ Authoritative   ☐ Authoritarian   ☐ Neglectful   ☐ Permissive
2. what type of parent is Veruca's father?
    ☐ Authoritative   ☐ Authoritarian   ☐ Neglectful   ☐ Permissive
3. what type of parent is your father/mother?
    ☐ Authoritative   ☐ Authoritarian   ☐ Neglectful   ☐ Permissive
4. which type of parenting style do you think is the best?
    ☐ Authoritative   ☐ Authoritarian   ☐ Neglectful   ☐ Permissive

5

The Chance Is Getting Smaller
Pages 26-34

Word Power

1. anxious *adj.* 焦慮的
2. strike lucky 意外得到好運
3. crane *v.* 伸長 (脖子)
4. brightly *adv.* 雀躍地

5. jostle *v.* 推擠
6. criticize *v.* 批評
7. solid *adj.* 不間斷的
8. despicable *adj.* 令人厭惡的

Reading Comprehension

( ) 1. What present does Charlie get for his birthday?
    (A) A Banana Fudge Slammer.
    (B) A Strawberry Everlasting Gobstopper.
    (C) A Nutty Crunch Surprise.
    (D) A Whipple-Scrumptious Fudgemallow Delight.

( ) 2. What does Violet do with her gum when she is eating?
    (A) She throws it away.
    (B) She puts it behind her ear.
    (C) She keeps chewing it at the same time as eating.
    (D) She puts an extra piece in her mouth.

( ) 3. What does "whiz-banger" mean on page 33?
    (A) Excellent.
    (B) Terrible.
    (C) Boring.
    (D) Noisy.

Further Discussion

1. Charlie's grandparents don't expect him to find the Golden Ticket. Imagine you were one of his grandparents. Write your thoughts about what you might think and say.

_____

_____

_____

_____

_____

_____

2. Violet loves attention. How do we know? Give textual evidence.

_____

_____

_____

_____

_____

_____

3. Mike loves gangster movies. Why do you think he likes them so much? What movies, TV shows or games do you think he may like to watch or play? Why?

_____

_____

_____

_____

_____

_____

Character Log

Take notes of each character's personal traits and try to draw a picture of each character with a pencil. You may need to come back here and add more details or alter the pictures when you read more of the novel.

Charlie Bucket
A small boy
Poor family
Loves chocolate
Polite
Skinny

Augustus Gloop

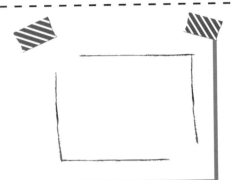

Veruca Salt

Violet Beauregarde

Mike Teavee

Grandpa Joe

Willy Wonka

Secret Workers

6

After the Final Try
Pages 34-46

Word Power

1. sly *adj.* (表情) 神祕的
2. vital *adj.* 重要的
3. desperate *adj.* 嚴峻的
4. exhaustion *n.* 筋疲力竭

5. shiver *v.* 發抖
6. bulge *v.* 鼓起
7. reach *v.* 伸手
8. enviously *adv.* 嫉妒地

Reading Comprehension

(　) 1. After Mr. Bucket loses his job, what does he do to make money?
    (A) He sells chocolate.
    (B) He delivers newspapers.
    (C) He shovels snow from the street.
    (D) He prepares cabbage soup.

(　) 2. What does Charlie **NOT** do to save energy when his family have no food?
    (A) He often lies in bed at home.
    (B) He sits quietly during recess.
    (C) He walks slowly to school.
    (D) He does everything slowly and carefully.

(　) 3. What does a man offer Charlie for his Golden Ticket?
    (A) A car.
    (B) A bicycle.
    (C) Food.
    (D) Clothes.

1. Grandpa Joe decides to spend his last money on finding the Golden Ticket. What might be the reasons for this decision? Do you agree with him?

_____

_____

_____

_____

_____

_____

2. Why does Charlie decide to buy another chocolate bar when he stares at the nine coins on the counter? What would you do if you were Charlie?

_____

_____

_____

_____

_____

_____

3. If you found the Golden Ticket like Charlie does and somebody offered you a lot of money for the Golden Ticket, what would you do? Why?

_____

_____

_____

_____

_____

_____

Happiness Line Chart

Charlie's emotions go up and down before he finds the Golden Ticket, and at the same time, he is starving. Describe how Charlie is feeling after each event, estimate his happiness scores and physical satisfaction scores, and then draw the line chart.

	Charlie's Feelings	Happiness Score (0–10)	Physical Satisfaction Score (0–10)
Event 1: Charlie finds out only one Golden Ticket is left.	Charlie is a little sad when he discovers that there is only one ticket left as he thinks he may not be able to meet Willy Wonka. But there is still a little hope, so he isn't distraught. Besides, he must have been starved because the family have been eating cabbage soup every day.	4	2
Event 2: Grandpa Joe buys a Nutty Crunch Surprise.			

Event 3: The weather turns very cold, and the family have no food.		
Event 4: Charlie finds a dollar in the snow.		
Event 5: Charlie buys and eats the Whipple-Scrumptious Fudgemallow Delight.		
Event 6: Charlie finds the Golden Ticket.		

7

Getting Ready to Go to the Factory
Pages 46–57

Pages 46–57

Word Power

1. verdict *n.* 判斷
2. conduct *v.* 帶領
3. fluster *v.* 使緊張
4. pandemonium *n.* 騷動，混亂

5. shield *v.* 保護
6. dreadful *adj.* 可怕的
7. fiend *n.* 瘋狂愛好者
8. rusty *adj.* 生鏽的

Reading Comprehension

(　) 1. What happens when Grandpa Joe finds out that Charlie has found the Golden Ticket?
    (A) He starts shouting and asks Charlie to give it to him.
    (B) He sits there and says nothing.
    (C) He knocks his bowl of soup over.
    (D) He falls out of bed and twists his ankle.

(　) 2. What are in the trucks which take Golden Ticket holders home after the tour of the factory?
    (A) Toys.
    (B) Gold.
    (C) Precious stones.
    (D) Delicious food.

(　) 3. When can the children go into the factory?
    (A) The first day of January.
    (B) The first day of February.
    (C) The last day of January.
    (D) The last day of February.

Further Discussion

1. The journalists all want to talk to Charlie after he finds the Golden Ticket. What would you tell them if you were Charlie?

_____

_____

_____

_____

_____

_____

2. How would you be feeling if you were one of the children going into the factory? What would you do to prepare?

_____

_____

_____

_____

_____

_____

3. People outside the gates of the factory give comments on the five children. What do they say? Do you think it is fair to give those comments?

_____

_____

_____

_____

_____

_____

Letter Writing

Imagine you were Charlie and wrote a letter to Willy Wonka thanking him for the Golden Ticket. Describe the way you were feeling about going to the factory.

8

Inside the Factory
Pages 57-68

Word Power

1. plum-colored *adj.* 紫紅色的
2. pump sb's hand 有力地握手
3. perish *v.* 喪生
4. corridor *n.* 走廊，通道

5. dawdle *v.* 磨蹭
6. warren *n.* 洞窟
7. can't abide sth 無法忍受⋯
8. staggered *adj.* 吃驚的

Reading Comprehension

(　　) 1. What **CAN'T** be smelled in the factory?
　　　(A) Mint.
　　　(B) Coffee.
　　　(C) Lemon peel.
　　　(D) Cigarettes.

(　　) 2. Roald Dahl describes the factory as a rabbit warren. Why?
　　　(A) The factory is like a maze.
　　　(B) The factory has many rabbits inside.
　　　(C) The factory has many doors.
　　　(D) The factory is above ground.

(　　) 3. What is the grass in the meadow made from?
　　　(A) Lollipops.
　　　(B) Mint chocolate.
　　　(C) Minty sugar.
　　　(D) Candy cane.

Further Discussion

1. Why do you think Willy Wonka is so excited to meet all the children?

_____

_____

_____

_____

_____

_____

2. Wonka says he can't "abide" ugliness. Explain three things you can't abide.

_____

_____

_____

_____

_____

_____

3. Why are there a waterfall and a meadow inside the chocolate room?

_____

_____

_____

_____

_____

_____

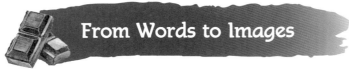

From Words to Images

According to Chapter 15, what does the chocolate room look like? Draw it below and try to include all the details from pages 63, 64 and 66.

Augustus Disappears and Oompa-Loompas Arrive
Pages 68–80

Word Power

1. import *v.* 引進，進口
2. infest *v.* (害蟲) 猖獗、橫行於
3. cacao bean *n.* 可可豆
4. interrupt *v.* 打斷
5. dive *v.* 跳水
6. stick *v.* 被困住
7. pull oneself together 冷靜下來
8. nincompoop *n.* 傻瓜

Reading Comprehension

( ) 1. How did Willy Wonka get the Oompa-Loompas over to his factory?
    (A) He took them on a truck.
    (B) He put them in packing cases.
    (C) He sent them by post.
    (D) They swam over.

( ) 2. What clothes do the male Oompa-Loompas wear?
    (A) Nothing.
    (B) Leaves.
    (C) Deerskins.
    (D) Tiger skins.

( ) 3. Why is Augustus deaf to everything except the call of his stomach?
    (A) He has a hearing problem.
    (B) He is very hungry.
    (C) He hates his parents and Willy Wonka.
    (D) He wants to drink as much chocolate as he can.

Further Discussion

1. What's Loompaland like?

_____

_____

_____

_____

_____

_____

2. When Augustus is going to stick in the pipe, someone says "It's a wonder to me how that pipe is big enough for him to go through it." Who is this speaker? What can we infer from these words?

_____

_____

_____

_____

_____

_____

_____

3. What is the Oompa-Loompas' song actually saying about Augustus Gloop?

_____

_____

_____

_____

_____

_____

The song "Augustus Gloop" has different versions. You can see the original version from pages 78–80. Please read it aloud.

The novel was first adapted into a musical film in 1971. Here is the 1971 version of "Augustus Gloop." Let's listen!

The second adaption of the novel was filmed in 2005, and it has a new version of "Augustus Gloop." Try to sing along!

What are the similarities among these three versions?
1. They have the same singers: _____
2. They have a common theme:

    _____

Oompa–Loompa
(Augustus) – Lyrics

Augustus Gloop.
Warner Bros.

But if Augustus himself has a chance to sing, what song would it be? Think about what Augustus may feel and think, and finish his song with the words below.

remain	pipe	nincompoop	smile	again	juvenile	body type

Augustus Gloop, Augustus Gloop,
My name doesn't mean a _____.
Augustus Gloop, I eat and _____,
Just like you every _____.

I want to change my _____!
Don't send me shooting up the _____!
My love for chocolate will still _____,
But I won't touch your chocolate _____.
I won't touch your chocolate again!

The song above can be sung to the melody of 2005 version of "Augustus Gloop." Let's sing for the poor greedy boy!

10

The Chocolate River Journey
Pages 80–91

Word Power

1. yacht *n.* 遊艇
2. a kick in the pants 教訓
3. hair cream *n.* 護髮霜
4. whip *n.* 鞭子 *v.* 攪拌

5. everlasting *adj.* 永恆的
6. toffee *n.* 太妃糖
7. suck *v.* 吸吮
8. stand back 退後

Reading Comprehension

( ) 1. What is Wonka's boat made from?
    (A) Glass.
    (B) Chocolate.
    (C) Boiled sweets.
    (D) Fudge.

( ) 2. What happens in the inventing room when the machine goes phut?
    (A) A green marble comes out.
    (B) A piece of chewing gum comes out.
    (C) A saucepan starts to sizzle.
    (D) An Everlasting Gobstopper comes out.

( ) 3. How long does it take hair to grow after one eats Hair Toffee?
    (A) 30 minutes
    (B) 1 hour
    (C) 1 hour 30 minutes
    (D) 3 hours

Further Discussion

1. Charlie talks about all the astonishments he has seen in the factory. What is the most astonishing thing you have seen or done and why?

_____

_____

_____

_____

_____

_____

2. While in the boat, the children pass Storeroom Number 54, which is full of different types of cream sweets. Imagine you went into the room. What would you see inside? What would you do and how would you feel?

_____

_____

_____

_____

_____

_____

3. Willy Wonka says "Don't argue" to Mike Teavee when he asks him a question about Hair Toffee. Why do you think he says so?

_____

_____

_____

_____

_____

_____

Cacao Bean Journey

While the children are making the factory journey by boat, let's go on a cacao bean journey on a map! The graph on the right shows the main trade flows of cacao beans. Color the cacao producing countries and the importers on the world map, and draw arrows to indicate the trade flows.

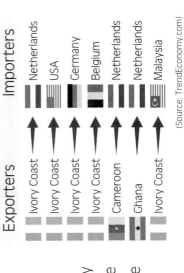

Exporters		Importers
Ivory Coast	→	Netherlands
Ivory Coast	→	USA
Ivory Coast	→	Germany
Ivory Coast	→	Belgium
Cameroon	→	Netherlands
Ghana	→	Netherlands
Ivory Coast	→	Malaysia

(Source: TrendEconomy.com)

11

Violet Turns Violet
Pages 91–102

Word Power

1. gleaming *adj.* 閃閃發光的
2. froth *v.* 起泡沫
3. strip *n.* 長條
4. tongs *n.* 鉗子

5. spit out 吐出
6. swell up 膨脹
7. wring one's hands 扭手
8. squeeze *v.* 擠壓，榨

Reading Comprehension

(　) 1. How does Willy Wonka make the chewing gum?
    (A) By melting plastic.
    (B) By freezing soda.
    (C) By mixing different liquids.
    (D) By heating blueberry juice.

(　) 2. Which of the following things will Wonka's chewing gum **NOT** remove?
    (A) Kitchens.
    (B) Groceries.
    (C) Plates.
    (D) Supermarkets.

(　) 3. Which part of Violet's body starts to turn blue first?
    (A) Her nose.
    (B) Her cheeks.
    (C) Her hair.
    (D) Her mouth.

Further Discussion

1. Would you like to have Wonka's chewing gum, which can replace a three course meal? Why or why not?

_____
_____
_____
_____
_____
_____

2. Find an example of a simile about Violet in Chapter 21. Try to write your own sentence using the simile.

_____
_____
_____
_____
_____
_____

3. Find three pairs of rhyming words from the song about Violet. Use them to write your own sentences that rhyme.

_____
_____
_____
_____
_____
_____

The History of Candy

Mr. Wonka invents "amazing" chewing gum. In the history of candy, there were indeed many inventions that amazed the world. Below are major historical events about candy. Think about when they happened and write A−F on the timeline.

A. Joseph Storrs Fry invented a way to grind cacao beans using a steam engine. This invention led to mass production of chocolate.

B. Spanish explorer Hernán Cortés overthrew the Aztec Empire and presented their chocolate drink to Charles V, the Holy Roman Emperor. The Spanish began to add sugar to the drink, and it became popular among the upper class.

2000 BC

The first candy was made from honey mixed with fruit by the ancient Egyptians.

250 BC

Mayans began to use cacao beans as money.

1521
(   )

1400 BC
(   )

1502
(   )

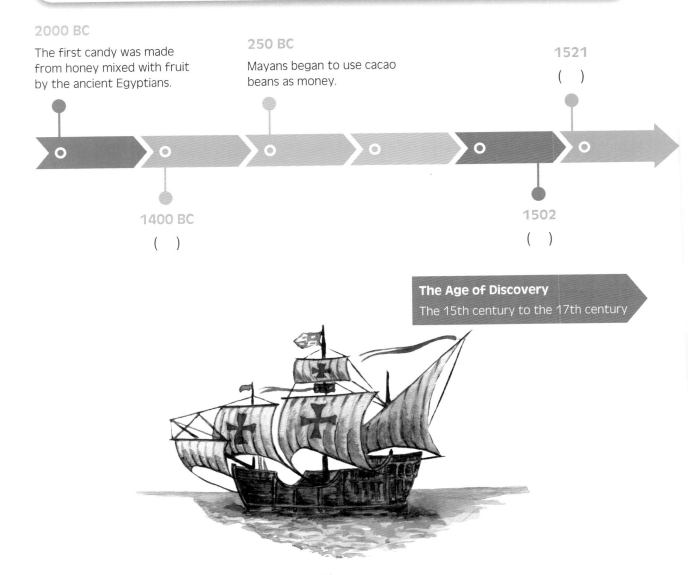

The Age of Discovery
The 15th century to the 17th century

36

C. In Mesoamerica, one of the ancient civilizations around the world, people drank unsweetened chocolate.

D. American soldiers ate special chocolate bars called D-bars to get energy during the Normandy landings. D-bars were invented by Hershey. They were high in calories and could withstand high temperatures.

E. During the First World War, the U.S. Army asked chocolate makers to produce 40 pounds blocks of chocolate, chopped them into small pieces, and distributed to the American soldiers in Europe.

F. Christopher Columbus carried first cacao beans to Europe from Central America.

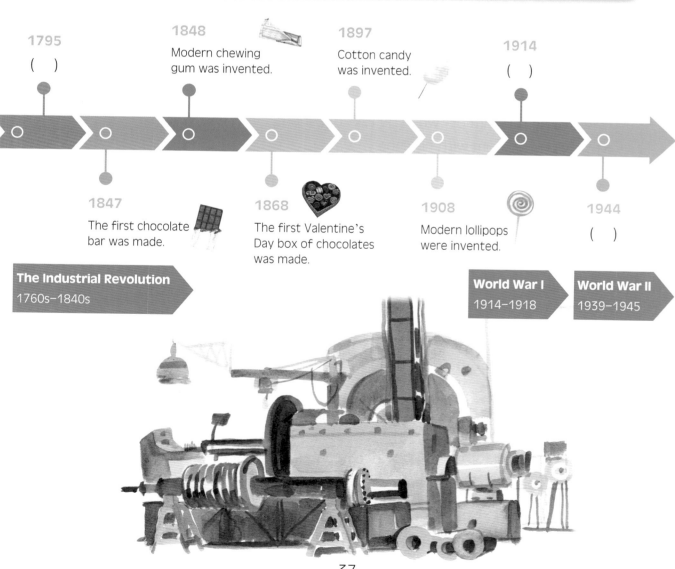

1795
(   )

1848
Modern chewing gum was invented.

1897
Cotton candy was invented.

1914
(   )

1847
The first chocolate bar was made.

1868
The first Valentine's Day box of chocolates was made.

1908
Modern lollipops were invented.

1944
(   )

The Industrial Revolution
1760s–1840s

World War I
1914–1918

World War II
1939–1945

37

Lifting Drinks and Square Candies
Pages 102-109

Word Power

1. mumble *v.* 咕噥
2. scuttle *v.* 碎步快跑
3. dash *v.* 急奔
4. burp *v.* / *n.* 打嗝

5. take a peek 看一眼
6. triumphantly *adv.* 得意洋洋地
7. whoop *v.* 高喊
8. bannister *n.* 欄杆

Reading Comprehension

(　) 1. Willy Wonka doesn't like Mike Teavee. How do we know?
    (A) He never smiles at him.
    (B) He tells him off when he asks questions.
    (C) He hits him with his cane.
    (D) He doesn't let him go in the Eatable Marshmallow Pillows room.

(　) 2. What color is Violet after she has been de-juiced?
    (A) Blue.
    (B) Green.
    (C) Purple.
    (D) Red.

(　) 3. What is the way to get down from the ceiling if you drink Fizzy Lifting Drinks?
    (A) To burp.
    (B) To fart.
    (C) You will fall down after five minutes.
    (D) You can't get down.

Further Discussion

1. Imagine you went into the Eatable Marshmallow Pillows room. Describe what it would be like. Use your senses.

_____

_____

_____

_____

_____

_____

2. If you could go in any of the rooms and try the candy inside, which one would you go in and why?

_____

_____

_____

_____

_____

_____

3. Why does Willy Wonka say that the square candies look round? Mrs. Salt doesn't believe him. What does she think?

_____

_____

_____

_____

_____

_____

More Than One Truth

In Chapter 23, the square candies look square, but also *look* round. In reality, people often see the same things from different angles, and like Mike Teavee and Veruca Salt, they think they are right and that others are wrong. They often forget there may be more than one truth.

Look at the six pictures below. What do you see? Write your answers and discuss with your classmates how things that are the same can be two different things.

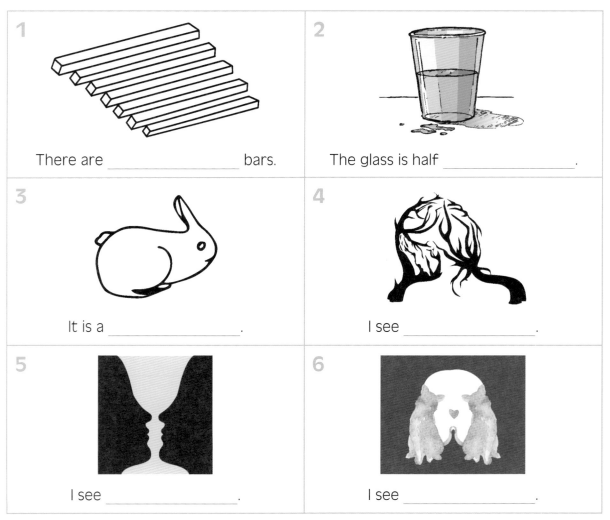

1
There are _____ bars.

2
The glass is half _____.

3
It is a _____.

4
I see _____.

5
I see _____.

6
I see _____.

13

Veruca Salt Disappears
Pages 109–118

Word Power

1. shell *n.* 殼 *v.* 剝殼
2. knuckle *n.* 指關節
3. hollow *adj.* 空的
4. chute *n.* 滑道，管槽

5. incinerator *n.* 焚化爐
6. peer *v.* 仔細看
7. tumble *v.* 跌倒
8. rancid *adj.* 有油耗味的

Reading Comprehension

(　　) 1. What do the squirrels shell?
    (A) Peas.
    (B) Peanuts.
    (C) Walnuts.
    (D) Cacao beans.

(　　) 2. Which animal does Veruca **NOT** have as a pet?
    (A) Dogs.
    (B) Mice.
    (C) Goldfish.
    (D) Snakes.

(　　) 3. How often do they turn the incinerator on in the factory?
    (A) Twice a day.
    (B) Every day.
    (C) Once every two days.
    (D) Twice a week.

Further Discussion

1. Why does Willy Wonka only use squirrels to take the walnuts out of their shells? Describe the process of the squirrels removing the walnuts from their shells and how they sort them.

_____

_____

_____

_____

_____

_____

2. Veruca wants a squirrel as a pet. Imagine you were her parents. What would you do or say to her?

_____

_____

_____

_____

_____

_____

3. Veruca doesn't like being told she can't do something because she is used to doing what she likes and she believes she is more important than everybody else. Do you know anyone like this, who thinks that they can always do what they like? Give examples of what they do, and why they think they are so important?

_____

_____

_____

_____

_____

Parents' Imperfections

Parents may do the wrong things and have negative influences on their children. Think about what the Oompa-Loompas sing in Chapter 24, and listen to Linkin Park's "Numb" and Sasha Sloan's "Older."

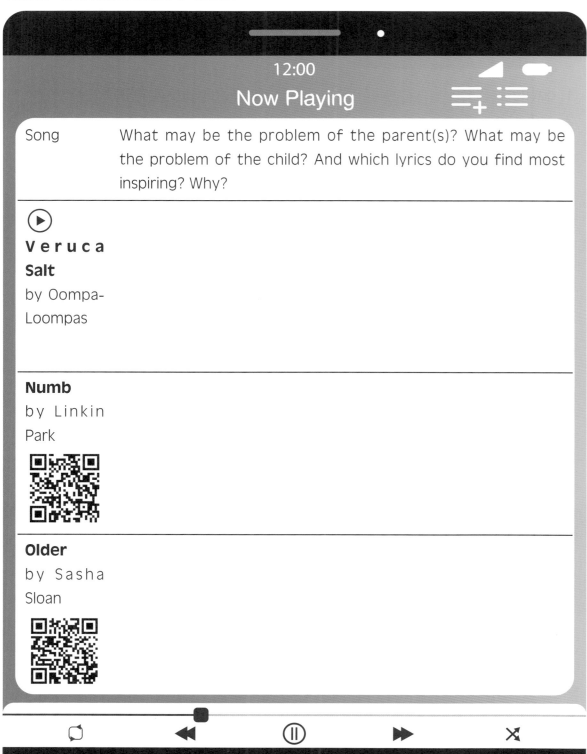

Song	What may be the problem of the parent(s)? What may be the problem of the child? And which lyrics do you find most inspiring? Why?
▶ **V e r u c a Salt** by Oompa-Loompas	
Numb by Linkin Park	
Older by Sasha Sloan	

14

The Glass Elevator and the TV Room
Pages 118−129

Word Power

1. cavity *n.* 蛀洞
2. collision *n.* 相撞
3. brake *n.* 剎車
4. gasp *v.* 喘氣

5. dazzlingly *adv.* 刺眼地
6. in small doses 短時間，一下子
7. switch *n.* 開關 *v.* 按開關
8. flicker *v.* 閃爍

Reading Comprehension

(　　) 1. Which is true about Wonka's elevator?
　　(A) It is made of steel.
　　(B) It can go only up and down.
　　(C) It can go to any room in the factory.
　　(D) It has only one button inside.

(　　) 2. What does Charlie **NOT** see while in the elevator?
　　(A) A caramel lake.
　　(B) A fudge mountain.
　　(C) A village of Oompa-Loompas.
　　(D) A candy school.

(　　) 3. Why are the Oompa-Loompas not laughing while they are in the Television-Chocolate room?
　　(A) They are angry with Willy Wonka.
　　(B) They know what they are doing is dangerous.
　　(C) They are upset that they can't all be on TV.
　　(D) They have to be quiet to make the experiment work.

Further Discussion

1. Which of the rooms that the elevator can visit sounds the most interesting to you? Why?

_____

_____

_____

_____

_____

_____

2. Mr. Wonka says Mike Teavee is a nice boy but he talks too much. Do you agree with Mr. Wonka? Why or why not?

_____

_____

_____

_____

_____

_____

3. If you could send something through a TV or computer screen, what would you send and why?

_____

_____

_____

_____

_____

_____

PEEL Writing

Today, people spend lots of time on screens, including not only televisions, but also computers, smart phones, tablets. . . . Do you think screen time is harmful or beneficial? Write a paragraph to express your opinion. You may use a "PEEL" structure to help you.

P	**E**	**E**	**L**
Point	**E**vidence	**E**xplanation	**L**ink
Make the main point for the paragraph.	Give an example to prove your point.	How does the evidence support your point?	Link back to the main point and set up the next point in the next paragraph.

Point

Evidence

Explanation

Link

15

Mike Teavee Is Shrunk
Pages 129–141

Word Power

1. nasty *adj.* 糟糕的
2. scatter *v.* 分散
3. glare *n.* 強光
4. midget *n.* 侏儒，矮子

5. wail *v.* 大哭
6. tread *v.* 踩 (-trod-trodden)
7. tantrum *n.* 發脾氣
8. don't mention it 不用謝

Reading Comprehension

(　　) 1. Why does Mike run so fast toward the great camera?
　　(A) He wants to be the first person in the world to be sent by TV.
　　(B) He sees gangsters with guns and wants to take a photo of them.
　　(C) He is too excited because he has never seen a camera before.
　　(D) Wonka asks him to pull down the switch of the camera immediately.

(　　) 2. What does Mike's father say he will do with the TV when he gets home?
　　(A) Give it away.
　　(B) Buy a new one.
　　(C) Smash it up.
　　(D) Throw it out the window.

(　　) 3. Which two vitamins does Wonka's Supervitamin Candy **NOT** have?
　　(A) Vitamin C and T.
　　(B) Vitamin E and U.
　　(C) Vitamin H and S.
　　(D) Vitamin J and K.

1. If you were Willy Wonka, what would you say to Mike Teavee to try to make him stop sending himself through the TV?

_____
_____
_____
_____
_____
_____

2. What does Roald Dahl think about TV? Use the text to explain what he thinks about it, and give three examples from the Oompa-Loompas' song to prove your viewpoint.

_____
_____
_____
_____
_____
_____

3. Wonka tells Mr. and Mrs. Teavee that they don't have to be worried because all the children will "come out in the wash." What do you expect will happen to the four children who have gone? Do you think they will come back safe and sound?

_____
_____
_____
_____
_____
_____

You Are the Director!

A movie studio wants to make a new film based on *Charlie and the Chocolate Factory*. They need a director to help them. Please put the following actions in the correct order. Draw these shots on the storyboard and add some dialogues on it.

Shot	Action
	Mike Teavee asks Mr. Wonka if a real person can be sent from one place to another by television.
	Mike Teavee runs toward the other end of the room where the great camera is standing.
	Mike Teavee becomes a midget on the screen.
1	Mike Teavee is excited at seeing a bar of chocolate being sent by television.
	Mike Teavee is gone.
	Mike Teavee pulls down the switch and leaps out into the full glare of the mighty lens.

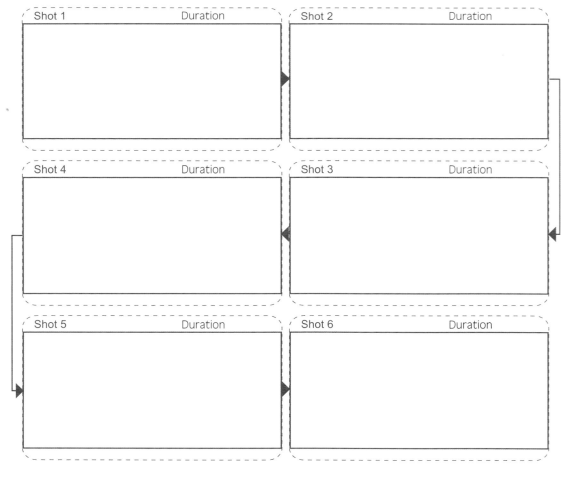

16

The Only One Left
Pages 142–147

1. have a hunch 有預感
2. fetch *v.* 接來，請來
3. after you 你先請
4. cling to 緊抓

5. long to 渴望
6. be tempted 想要
7. crash *v.* 撞擊發生巨響
8. hover *v.* 盤旋

Reading Comprehension

(　) 1. What does Wonka do to show excitement about Charlie's victory?
    (A) He jumps up and down.
    (B) He shakes Charlie's hand furiously.
    (C) He spins around.
    (D) He gives Charlie a huge bag of candy.

(　) 2. What happens when Wonka presses the "UP AND OUT" button?
    (A) Charlie shoots out the top of the elevator.
    (B) The elevator goes out the factory roof.
    (C) The bottom of the elevator opens and they all fall out.
    (D) Everybody falls on the floor because the elevator goes so quickly.

(　) 3. What does Grandpa Joe think when the elevator hits the roof?
    (A) The elevator is strong enough.
    (B) The factory is going to explode.
    (C) They are going to die.
    (D) People will come to their rescue.

Further Discussion

1. Why do you think Willy Wonka says he had a hunch at the start that Charlie would be the winner?

_____

_____

_____

_____

_____

_____

2. Why is Charlie not frightened when he knows Wonka is going to do something crazy?

_____

_____

_____

_____

_____

_____

3. Wonka says he has been longing to press the "UP AND OUT" button for years. Why has he never done it until now? Is there anything you have been longing to do for a while? Why don't you do it?

_____

_____

_____

_____

_____

_____

Charlie's Profile Page

Below is Charlie's profile page on social media. Finish his personal information and think of what comments other characters may leave below Charlie's post.

Charlie Bucket
I'm pleased to meet you.

| Posts | About | Friends | Photos | Check-Ins | More ▼ |

Intro

🏠 Lives in a great town

📍 Visited Wonka's Chocolate Factory

👥 Became friends with Willy Wonka and 4 other people

🔊 Followed by readers around the world

Family

_____

_____

_____

_____

_____

Posts   Filters

Charlie Bucket
February 1 at 4:20 PM 🌐

Something crazy is going to happen now! Mr. Wonka says I've won! I've no idea where he is going to take us, but I'm not afraid or nervous. I'm just excited!!

👍 Like   💬 Comment   ➡ Share

Willy Wonka
_____

Joe Bucket
_____

Augustus Gloop
_____

Violet Beauregarde
_____

Veruca Salt
_____

Mike Teavee

17

The End
Pages 147–155

Word Power

1. careless *adj.* 粗心的
2. gaze *v.* 凝視
3. run *v.* 經營，管理
4. sensible *adj.* 理智的

5. despair *v.* 絕望
6. cement *n.* 水泥
7. be in ruins 成為廢墟
8. petrified *adj.* 僵住的

Reading Comprehension

( ) 1. What does Mike Teavee look like after he leaves the factory?
   (A) A TV.
   (B) A blueberry.
   (C) A pile of garbage.
   (D) A wire.

( ) 2. What thing does **NOT** happen when the elevator crashes through the Buckets' roof?
   (A) Grandma Georgina jumps out of bed.
   (B) Grandma Josephine drops her false teeth.
   (C) Mr. Bucket rushes in to see what is happening.
   (D) Grandpa George hides his head under the blanket.

( ) 3. How does Charlie get all his family to come with him to the factory?
   (A) He promises them they will have another house.
   (B) He says he will pay them with Wonka's fortune if they come.
   (C) He tells them about his lifetime supply of candy.
   (D) He puts the grandparents' bed in the elevator.

Further Discussion

1. Why does Willy Wonka want a child to take over and run his factory, not a grown-up?

_____

_____

_____

_____

_____

2. If you were Charlie, and you were given the factory, what would you do as the factory owner? Why?

_____

_____

_____

_____

_____

_____

3. If you could rewrite the book and have a different ending, what would you change and how?

_____

_____

_____

_____

_____

_____

Character Word Cloud

Willy Wonka is a complicated character. He has many different sides to his personality. After finishing reading this novel, what do you know about him? Come up with at least 20 characteristics of Willy Wonka. Use these words to create a shape that you think can represent him.

Willy Wonka's characteristics:

eccentric

18

Overall Review

Book Review

After reading the novel, try to write a review like a professional book critic.
My Rating:

1. What are the themes of the book?

_____

_____

_____

_____

_____

_____

2. Give a recommendation, e.g. "If you like. . . , you will love this book," or "I
   recommend this book to anyone who. . . ."

_____

_____

_____

_____

_____

_____

Book Blurb

Suppose you were designing a new back cover for the book. How would you write the blurb? Tell about the book, but don't reveal too much. You need to intrigue the readers.

◆ Wonder 解讀攻略

戴逸群 編著／Joseph E. Schier 審閱

Lexile 藍思分級：790

☞ 議題：品德教育、生命教育、家庭教育、閱讀素養

◆ Love, Simon 解讀攻略

戴逸群 主編／林冠瑋 編著／Ian Fletcher 審閱

Lexile 藍思分級：640

☞ 議題：性別平等、人權教育、多元文化、閱讀素養

◆ Matilda 解讀攻略

戴逸群 主編／林佳紋 編著／Joseph E. Schier 審閱

Lexile 藍思分級：840

☞ 議題：性別平等、人權教育、家庭教育、閱讀素養

◆ 英文小說解讀攻略：奇幻篇

戴逸群 主編／簡嘉妤 編著／Ian Fletcher 審閱

Lexile 藍思分級：880

☞ 議題：品德教育、家庭教育、多元文化、閱讀素養

◆ 英文小說解讀攻略：生命篇

戴逸群 主編／陳思安 編著／Ian Fletcher 審閱

Lexile 藍思分級：550

☞ 議題：生命教育、性別平等、人權教育、閱讀素養

Answer Key

Lesson 1
Reading Comprehension
1. (B)   2. (C)   3. (C)

Lesson 2
Reading Comprehension
1. (B)   2. (C)   3. (A)

Lesson 3
Reading Comprehension
1. (A)   2. (C)   3. (D)

Lesson 4
Reading Comprehension
1. (D)   2. (A)   3. (C)

Different Types of Parenting Styles
1. Permissive
2. Permissive

Lesson 5
Reading Comprehension
1. (D)   2. (B)   3. (A)

Lesson 6
Reading Comprehension
1. (C)   2. (A)   3. (B)

Lesson 7
Reading Comprehension
1. (C)   2. (D)   3. (B)

Lesson 8
Reading Comprehension
1. (D)   2. (A)   3. (C)

Lesson 9
Reading Comprehension
1. (B)   2. (C)   3. (D)

Sing and Sympathize
1. Oompa-Loompas
2. Augustus Gloop is greedy and is taking the consequences.
* nincompoop, smile, juvenile, body type, pipe, remain, again

Lesson 10
Reading Comprehension
1. (C)   2. (D)   3. (A)

Cacao Bean Journey

Lesson 11
Reading Comprehension
1. (C)   2. (D)   3. (A)

The History of Candy
(C) (F) (B) (A) (E) (D)

Lesson 12
Reading Comprehension
1. (B)   2. (C)   3. (A)

More Than One Truth
1. 5 / 7
2. empty / full
3. rabbit / duck
4. two trees / a girl
5. two faces / a goblet
6. two cats / a dog

Lesson 13
Reading Comprehension
1. (C)   2. (D)   3. (C)

Lesson 14

Reading Comprehension

1. (C) 2. (D) 3. (B)

Lesson 15

Reading Comprehension

1. (A) 2. (D) 3. (C)

You Are the Director!

2, 3, 6, 1, 5, 4

Lesson 16

Reading Comprehension

1. (B) 2. (B) 3. (C)

Charlie's Profile Page

Family: Joe Bucket, Josephine Bucket,
George, Georgina, Mr. Bucket,
Mrs. Bucket

Lesson 17

Reading Comprehension

1. (D) 2. (A) 3. (D)